Disney · PIXAR

Cars 3

Read-Along
STORYBOOK AND CD

This is a story about Lightning McQueen and his love for racing. You will know it's time to turn the page when you hear this sound. . . . Let's begin now.

Materials and characters from the movie *Cars 3*. Copyright © 2017 Disney Enterprises, Inc. and Pixar. All rights reserved. Disney/Pixar elements © Disney/Pixar; rights in underlying vehicles are the property of the following third parties: AMC, El Camino, Gremlin, Hudson, Hudson Hornet, Nash Ambassador, Pacer, Plymouth Superbird and Willys are trademarks of FCA US LLC.; Dodge®, Jeep® and the Jeep® grille design are trademarks of FCA US LLC.; Darrell Waltrip marks used by permission of Darrell Waltrip Motor Sports; FIAT is a trademark of FCA Group Marketing S.p.A.; Fairlane, Ford Coupe, Mercury, Model T, and Mustang are trademarks of Ford Motor Company; Cadillac Coupe DeVille, Chevrolet, Chevrolet Impala, Corvette and Monte Carlo are trademarks of General Motors; Mack is a trademark of Mack Trucks, Inc.; Carrera and Porsche are trademarks of Porsche; Sarge's rank insignia design used with the approval of the U.S. Army; Volkswagen trademarks, design patents and copyrights are used with the approval of the owner Volkswagen AG; background inspired by the Cadillac Ranch by Ant Farm (Lord, Michels and Marquez) © 1974. Published by Disney Press, an imprint of Disney Book Group. No part of this book may be reproduced or transmitted in any form or by any means, electronic or mechanical, including photocopying, recording, or by any information storage and retrieval system, without written permission from the publisher.

For information address Disney Press, 1101 Flower Street, Glendale, California 91201.

Printed in the United States of America

First Paperback Edition, May 2017   10 9 8 7 6 5 4 3 2 1

Library of Congress Control Number: 2016938189

ISBN 978-1-4847-8134-0

FAC-008598-17076

For more Disney Press fun, visit www.disneybooks.com

Disney PRESS
Los Angeles • New York

SUSTAINABLE FORESTRY INITIATIVE

Certified Chain of Custody
At Least 20% Certified Forest Content
www.sfiprogram.org
SFI-00993

Logo Applies to Text Stock Only

It was the first race of the season. Fans cheered as the cars headed toward the finish line. Out in front was number 95, Lightning McQueen. Lightning's friends Bobby Swift, Cal Weathers, and Brick Yardley followed close behind.

With a final burst of speed, Lightning surged past the finish line for the win! *"Ka-chow!"*

Lightning's season was off to a great start, and he kept winning races. Then, at the Motor Speedway of the South, all this changed. Bobby Swift was nose to nose with Lightning when, suddenly, an unknown race car blew by them. It was Jackson Storm, a rookie racer. Bobby and Lightning tried to regain their lead, but Storm won!

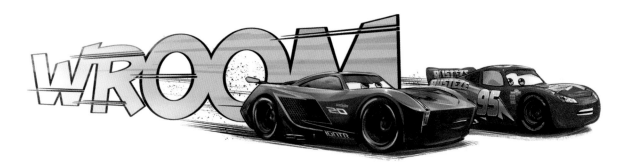

After the race, Lightning congratulated the rookie. "Hey, Jackson Storm, right? Great race today."

Storm grinned. "Oh, wow, thank you, Mr. McQueen. You have no idea what a pleasure it is for me to finally beat you."

"Oh, thanks!" Lightning turned away and then stopped. "Wait, hang on. Did you say 'meet,' or **'beat'**?"

Storm smirked. "I think you heard me."

Jackson Storm was part of a new generation of high-tech race cars. These Next Gen racers were faster than the cars that had come before. **They won race after race!**

Soon veteran racers began retiring or losing their sponsors. Lightning couldn't keep up with the Next Gens. In every race, he finished behind Storm. But he wasn't ready to give up and retire.

At the start of the final race of the season, Storm mocked Lightning. "Hey, Champ, where'd all your friends go?"

Lightning was determined to beat the Next Gen. When the racers began the last lap of the race, Storm passed Lightning to take the lead. Lightning pushed himself harder than ever. "Come on. Come on. **Come on!**"

Suddenly, Lightning pushed himself too hard. His tire blew out! As Lightning rolled over and over, his whole world went black.

In the months that followed, Lightning recovered from the crash. He was physically ready to race again, but he wondered if maybe it was time to retire.

Lightning thought about his mentor, Doc Hudson. Doc was one of the best racers of his time. But a devastating crash had ended his racing career early. Lightning made a choice. He wasn't going to end up like Doc. **"I decide when I'm done."**

When Lightning told his sponsors, Rusty and Dusty Rust-eze, that he would race again next season, they were thrilled. They had just made a deal to get Lightning a new training center so he could train on the same equipment as the Next Gens! But to do it, they had sold Rust-eze to a business car named Sterling. Rusty and Dusty introduced Lightning to his new sponsor. Sterling was excited to meet him.

"**Lightning McQueen**! You have no idea how much I've been looking forward to this."

Sterling took Lightning on a tour of the facility. Lightning watched in awe as a sleek yellow race car zoomed through a simulated course. Curious, he turned to Sterling. "Who's the racer?"

"No, no, no, no, she's a trainer." Sterling gestured toward the car. "**Cruz Ramirez**, best trainer in the business."

Sterling introduced the two of them. Cruz wasn't impressed by Lightning. "He looks old and broken down, with flabby tires."

Lightning was offended. "Hey, I do not!"

Cruz smiled. "Use that!"

Lightning laughed. "Oh, I see. I can use that energy for motivation, right? *Rarr*."

Over the next few weeks, Cruz led Lightning through a series of training exercises. She didn't think Lightning was ready for the simulator. Lightning disagreed. He hopped on the simulator—and crashed through its screen! Sterling thought Lightning's racing career was over. He wanted Lightning to **retire**.

Lightning pleaded for one last chance. "Look, I can do this. I promise! **I'll train like I did with Doc!**"

Sterling was skeptical. "One race? If you don't win at Florida, you'll retire?"

Lightning agreed. "Thank you, Mr. Sterling. You won't be sorry."

Lightning headed to Fireball Beach to restart his training. Cruz went along to track his speed. Lightning thought if he trained the same way he had with Doc, he would improve. "All right. Quicker than quick, faster than fast, **I am speed.**"

Cruz smiled at him. "That is great self-motivation. Did you come up with that?"

Lightning smiled proudly. "Yes, I did." Then he tore down the beach.

Cruz was supposed to be right beside him, tracking his speed, but she was stuck at the starting line, spinning her wheels. Cruz had never raced on sand before. Lightning gave her some tips. Cruz tried, but she spun out, stopped for passing crabs, and did doughnuts in the sand. Finally, she got it, and they were soon zooming across the beach. But Lightning's top speed was still slower than Jackson Storm's.

Lightning decided he needed to train against other racers on a dirt track, so he and Cruz went to the Thunder Hollow Speedway. Lightning disguised himself and signed up for the next race.

It wasn't until the gates closed that the two realized that it wasn't a traditional race. It was the **Thunder Hollow Crazy Eight** demolition derby, where cars smashed into each other. Cruz watched from the infield until the cars came after her, too.

Everyone—especially the undefeated champion, Miss Fritter—wanted a piece of the newcomers!

Lightning swerved to avoid crashing. Cruz was terrified! She tried hiding behind a stack of tires, but Miss Fritter had Cruz in her sights. Lightning shouted racing tips to Cruz and drew Miss Fritter away from her. At the end of the race, **Cruz was declared the winner!**

After the race, Lightning lashed out at Cruz. He still hadn't improved his speed, because he was too busy taking care of her. "This is my last chance, Cruz. Last! Final! Finito! If I lose, I never get to do this again! If you were a **racer**, you'd know what I'm talking about. **But you're not, so you don't!**"

Cruz turned away. "I've wanted to become a racer forever! **Because of you!**" Cruz told Lightning about her first big race. A local track owner had given her a chance at professional racing, and she'd blown it. She had been intimidated by the other racers. "I knew I could never compete. I just left. It was my one shot, and I didn't take it."

Lightning apologized. He hadn't meant to hurt Cruz's feelings.

The next day, Cruz resigned as Lightning's trainer. But Lightning asked her to come with him to the famous Thomasville Speedway. Lightning wanted Doc's old crew chief, Smokey, to train him. Cruz agreed. When they got there, they found Smokey. He took them to meet Doc's old friends. Lightning couldn't believe that he was actually meeting his heroes. "Three of the **biggest racing legends ever**: Junior 'Midnight' Moon, River Scott, Louise 'Barnstormer' Nash."

Later, Lightning admitted to Smokey that he didn't want to end up the same way Doc had. Smokey led Lightning to his garage. The letters Doc had sent him while he was Lightning's crew chief hung on the wall. Doc had seen something in Lightning that he didn't see in himself.

Smokey smiled. "Racing wasn't the best part of Hud's life— **you were.**"

Smokey agreed to train Lightning if he faced the facts. "You're old. Accept it. You'll never be as fast as Storm. **But you can be smarter than him.**"

Lightning needed someone to stand in as Jackson Storm during his training. Smokey thought Cruz was the natural choice. In the garage, the Legends modified Cruz for racing. She revved her engine excitedly and practiced her trash talking. "Oh, **you're going DOWN, McQueen!**"

Smokey trained Lightning the same way he had trained Doc Hudson. The other Legends helped, too. They did sprints and drills. Smokey tested Lightning's strength and torque by having him pull a heavy trailer. To practice getting through a crowd of racers, Smokey put Lightning and Cruz in a field of stampeding tractors! He was hard on Lightning. "Do you even want to be out here? **You gotta work harder!**"

After several weeks of training, it was nearly time for the big race. But Smokey had one more test for Lightning—an **all-out race against Cruz.**

The two stayed close together around the track. As they neared the finish line, Lightning gave it everything he had. But it wasn't enough. With a burst of speed, Cruz crossed the line ahead of him. "Woo-hoo! Yes! **That was awesome!** Woo!" Cruz stopped as she looked at Lightning. He was stunned that he had lost.

Finally, the day of the Florida 500 race arrived! As Lightning got into position, he felt nervous. He still hadn't managed to match Storm's speed, and his whole racing career was on the line.

The starting flag dropped, and the race began. As Lightning sped past the other cars, Smokey and Cruz cheered him on over the headset. Suddenly, Lightning heard Sterling tell Cruz to head back to the training center and take off the spoiler and racing tires— **she was a trainer, not a racer.**

Lightning had said the same thing. But he realized he was wrong. Cruz was awesome on the simulator, on the beach, and on the track at Thomasville. She'd always been a racer at heart— **she just needed a chance!**

Suddenly, there was a wreck on the track! Lightning immediately headed for the pit and asked Cruz to meet him there. The pit crew started working on Lightning, but he stopped them. He nodded toward Cruz. "Not me, her."

The crew gave Cruz new tires, a paint job—and the number 95. Cruz was completely confused. "Why are you doing this?"

Lightning smiled. He wanted to give her the chance to show the world that she was a racer.

As Cruz sped around the track, Lightning gave Smokey advice to pass along to her. Finally, Smokey gave Lightning the crew chief headset. Lightning coached Cruz around the track, reminding her of all she had learned. "Sneak through the window!"

Cruz saw an opening between racers and shot through. The crowd began cheering for the **new 95!**

With only a few laps left, Cruz moved up until she was just one car behind the leader—**Jackson Storm!**

Storm dropped back to taunt Cruz and her new paint job. He didn't think she deserved to be in the race. She wasn't a race car. **"You'll never be one of us."**

Storm's words hit Cruz hard, and she slowed down, falling behind Storm. He surged ahead. But Lightning wasn't going to let Cruz give up. "He sees something in you that you don't even see in yourself— that **you're a racer.** You made me believe it, but now you got to believe it, too. Use that!"

Cruz felt her confidence return and sped up until she was right behind Storm.

The Next Gen was rattled. **"You're not gonna win!"**

Cruz laughed at his frustration. "You know, you can use that anger to push through."

"I SAID I'M NOT ANGRY!"

Just then, Cruz made a move to the outside. Storm viciously slammed into her, pushing Cruz into the wall. "You don't belong on this track!"

Cruz wasn't going to give up. **"YES, I DO!"** She pushed herself off the wall and flipped over Storm! Cruz came down in first place and sprinted for the finish line!

Cruz won and the crowd went wild! The leader board showed the winner as "McQueen/Cruz." Because they had both raced wearing the number 95, Lightning and Cruz had both won. Lightning couldn't have been prouder of his friend.

Sterling couldn't believe it, either—Lightning didn't have to retire!

Back in Radiator Springs, Lightning and Cruz raced around Willys Butte. Cruz was now part of Tex Dinoco's race team and had taken Doc Hudson's old number, 51. Even better, Tex had bought Rust-eze from Sterling. **Lightning and Cruz were teammates!**

Lightning was happy. He knew that whether or not he raced again was up to him—and nobody else. But right now, all Lightning was focused on was getting Cruz ready for her next race.